THE JUMPING FROG

THE JUMPING FROG

*In English. Then in French. Then Clawed
Back into a Civilized Language Once More
by Patient, Unremunerated Toil.*

MARK TWAIN

Wood engravings by Alan James Robinson

MOYER BELL

WAKEFIELD, RHODE ISLAND & LONDON

Moyer Bell edition 1993.

Copyright © 1985 by Press of the Sea Turtle

LIBRARY OF CONGRESS
CATALOGING-IN-PUBLICATION DATA

Twain, Mark, 1835-1910.
[Celebrated jumping frog of Calaveras County.
French & English]
The jumping frog: in English, then in French, then clawed back into a civilized language once more by patient, unremunerated toil/Mark Twain; wood engravings by Alan James Robinson.

p. cm.
ISBN 1-55921-097-4
1. Frogs—California—Calaveras County—Fiction. 2. Calaveras County (Calif.)—Fiction. I. Title.
PS1322.C4 1993   93-13226
813'.4—dc20   CIP

Printed in the United States of America. Distributed in North America by Publishers Group West, P.O. Box 8843, Emeryville CA 94662 800-788-3123 (in California 510-658-3453) and in Europe by Gazelle Book Services Ltd., Falcon House, Queen Square, Lancaster LA1 1RN England 524-68765.

for Harold

Tom —

from his mother
who loves him.

December 3, 1996.

THE JUMPING FROG

THE JUMPING FROG*

IN ENGLISH. THEN IN FRENCH. THEN CLAWED
BACK INTO A CIVILIZED LANGUAGE ONCE MORE
BY PATIENT, UNREMUNERATED TOIL.

EVEN A CRIMINAL IS ENTITLED TO FAIR PLAY;
and certainly when a man who has done no harm has
been unjustly treated, he is privileged to do his best to
right himself. My attention has just been called to an
article some three years old in a French Magazine entitled, "Revue des Deux Mondes" (Review of Some
Two Worlds), wherein the writer treats of "Les Hu-
moristes Americaines" (These Humorists Americans).
I am one of these humorists Americans dissected by
him, and hence the complaint I am making.

This gentleman's article is an able one (as articles go,
in the French, where they always tangle up everything
to that degree that when you start into a sentence you
never know whether you are going to come out alive or
not). It is a very good article, and the writer says all
manner of kind and complimentary things about me—
for which I am sure I thank him with all my heart; but

*Written about 1865.

then why should he go and spoil all his praise by one unlucky experiment? What I refer to is this: he says my Jumping Frog is a funny story, but still he can't see why it should ever really convulse any one with laughter — and straightway proceeds to translate it into French in order to prove to his nation that there is nothing so very extravagantly funny about it. Just there is where my complaint originates. He has not translated it at all; he has simply mixed it all up; it is no more like the Jumping Frog when he gets through with it than I am like a meridian of longitude. But my mere assertion is no proof; wherefore I print the French version, that all may see that I do not speak falsely; furthermore, in order that even the unlettered may know my injury and give me their compassion, I have been at infinite pains and trouble to re-translate this French version back into English; and to tell the truth I have well nigh worn myself out at it, having scarcely rested from my work during five days and nights. I cannot speak the French language, but I can translate very well, though not fast, I being self-educated. I ask the reader to run his eye over the original English version of the Jumping Frog, and then read the French or my re-translation, and kindly take notice how the Frenchman has riddled the grammar. I think it is the worst I ever saw; and yet the French are called a polished nation. If I had a boy that put sentences together as they do, I would polish him to some purpose. Without further introduction, the Jumping Frog, as I originally wrote it, was as follows [after it will be found the French version, and after the latter my re-translation from the French]:

THE NOTORIOUS JUMPING FROG OF CALAVERAS* COUNTY.

In compliance with the request of a friend of mine, who wrote me from the East, I called on good-natured, garrulous old Simon Wheeler, and inquired after my friend's friend, Leonidas W. Smiley, as requested to do, and I hereunto append the result. I have a lurking suspicion that *Leonidas W.* Smiley is a myth; that my friend never knew such a personage; and that he only conjectured that if I asked old Wheeler about him, it would remind him of his infamous *Jim* Smiley, and he would go to work and bore me to

*Pronounced Cal-e-*va*-ras.

death with some exasperating reminiscence of him as long as and tedious as it should be useless to me. If that was the design, it succeeded.

I found Simon Wheeler dozing comfortably by the barroom stove of the dilapidated tavern in the decayed mining camp of Angel's, and I noticed that he was fat and bald-headed, and had an expression of winning gentleness and simplicity upon his tranquil countenance. He roused up, and gave me good-day. I told him a friend of mine had commissioned me to make some inquiries about a cherished companion of his boyhood named *Leonidas W.* Smiley—*Rev. Leonidas W.* Smiley, a young minister of the Gospel, who he had heard was at one time a resident of Angel's Camp. I added that if Mr. Wheeler could tell me anything about this Rev. Leonidas W. Smiley, I would feel under many obligations to him.

Simon Wheeler backed me into a corner and blockaded me there with his chair, and then sat down and reeled off the monotonous narrative which follows this paragraph. He never smiled, he never frowned, he never changed his voice from the gentle-flowing key to which he tuned his initial sentence, he never betrayed the slightest suspicion of enthusiasm; but all through the interminable narrative there ran a vein of impressive earnestness and sincerity, which showed me plainly that, so far from his imagining that there was anything ridiculous or funny about his story, he regarded it as a really important matter, and admired its two heroes as men of transcendent genius in *finesse*. I let him go on in his own way, and never interrupted him once.

"Rev. Leonidas W. H'm, Reverend Le—well, there was a feller here once by the name of *Jim* Smiley, in the winter of '49—or may be it was the spring of '50—I don't recollect exactly, somehow, though what makes me think it was one or the other is because I remember the big flume warn't finished when he first come to the camp; but any way, he was the curiosest man about always betting on anything that turned up you ever see, if he could get anybody to bet on the other side; and if he couldn't he'd change sides. Any way that suited the other man would suit *him*—any way just so's he got a bet, *he* was satisfied. But still he was lucky, uncommon lucky; he most always come out winner. He was always ready and laying for a chance; there couldn't be no solit'ry thing mentioned but that feller'd offer to bet on it, and take ary side you please, as I was just telling you. If there was a horse-race, you'd find him flush or you'd find him busted at the end of it; if there was a dog-fight, he'd bet on it; if there was a cat-fight, he'd bet on it; if there was a chicken-fight, he'd bet on it; why, if there was two birds setting on a fence, he would bet you which one would fly first; or if there was a camp-meeting, he would be there reg'lar to bet on Parson Walker, which he judged to be the best exhorter about here, and so he was too, and a good man. If he even see a straddle-bug start to go anywheres, he would bet you how long it would take him to get to—to wherever he was going to, and if you took him up, he would foller that straddle-bug to Mexico but what he would find out where he was bound for and how long he was on the road. Lots of the boys here has seen that Smiley, and can tell you about him. Why, it never made no difference to *him*—he'd bet on *any* thing—the dangdest feller. Parson Walker's wife laid very sick once, for a good while, and it seemed as if they warn't going to save her; but one morning he come in, and Smiley up and asked him how she was, and he said she was considable better— thank the Lord for his inf'-nite mercy—and coming on so smart that with the bless-ing of Prov'dence she'd get well yet; and Smiley, before he thought, says, "Well, I'll resk two-and-a-half she don't anyway."

Thish-yer Smiley had a mare—the boys called her the fifteen-minute nag, but that was only in fun, you know, because of course she was faster than that—and he used to win money on that horse, for all she was so slow and always had the asthma, or the distemper or the consumption, or something of that kind. They used to give her two or three hundred yards start, and then pass her under way; but always at the fag end of the race she'd get excited and desperate like, and come cavorting and straddling up, and scattering her legs around limber, sometimes in the air, and sometimes out to one side among the fences, and kicking up m-o-r-e dust and raising m-o-r-e racket with her coughing and sneezinz and blowing her nose—and *always* fetch up at the stand just about a neck ahead, as near as you could cipher it down.

And he had a little small bull-pup, that to look at him you'd think he warn't worth a cent but to set around and look ornery and lay for a chance to steal something. But as soon as money was up on him he was a different dog; his under-jaw'd begin to stick out like the fo'castle of a steamboat, and his teeth would uncover and shine like the furnaces. And a dog might tackle him and bully-rag him, and bite him, and throw him over his shoulder two or three times, and Andrew Jackson—which was the name of the pup— Andrew Jackson would never let on but what *he* was satisfied, and hadn't expected nothing else—and the bets being doubled and doubled on the other side all the time, till the money was all up; and then all of a sudden he would grab that other dog jest by the j'int of his hind leg and freeze to it—not chaw, you understand, but only just grip and hang on till they throwed up the sponge, if it was a year. Smiley always come out winner on that pup, till he harnessed a dog once that didn't have no hind legs, because they'd been sawed off in a circular saw, and when the thing had gone along far enough, and the money was all up, and he come to make a snatch for his pet holt, he see in a minute how he'd been imposed on, and how the other dog had him in the door, so to speak, and he 'peared surprised, and then he looked sorter discouraged-like, and didn't try no more to win the fight, and so he got shucked out bad. He give Smiley a look, as much as to say his heart was broke, and it was *his* fault, for putting up a dog that hadn't no hind legs for him to take holt of, which was his main dependence in a fight, and then he limped off a piece and laid down and died. It was a good pup, was that Andrew Jackson, and would have made a name for hisself if he'd lived, for the stuff was in him and he had genius—I know it, because he hadn't no opportunities to speak of, and it don't stand to reason that a dog could make such a fight as he could under them circumstances if he hadn't no talent. It always makes me feel sorry when I think of that last fight of his'n, and the way it turned out.

Well, thish-yer Smiley had rat-tarriers, and chicken cocks, and tomcats and all them kind of things, till you couldn't rest, and you couldn't fetch nothing for him to bet on but he'd match you. He ketched a frog one day, and took him home, and said he cal'lated to educate him; and so he never done nothing for three months but set in his back yard and learn that frog to jump. And you bet you he *did* learn him, too. He'd give him a little punch behind, and the next minute you'd see that frog whirling in the air like a doughnut —see him turn one summerset, or may be a couple, if he got a good start, and come down flat-footed and all right, like a cat. He got him up so in the matter of ketching flies, and kep' him in practice so constant, that he'd nail a fly every time as fur as he could see him. Smiley said all a frog wanted was education, and he could do 'most anything—and I believe him. Why, I've seen him set Dan'l Webster down here on this floor—Dan'l Webster was the name of the frog— and sing out, "Flies, Dan'l, flies!" and quicker'n you could wink he'd spring straight up and snake a fly off'n the counter there, and flop down on the floor ag'in as solid as a gob of mud, and fall to scratching the side of his head with his hind foot as indifferent as if he hadn't no idea he'd been doin' any more'n any frog might do. You never see a frog so modest and straightfor'ard as he was, for all he was so gifted. And when it come to fair and square jumping on a dead level, he could get over more ground at one straddle than any animal of his breed you ever see. Jumping on a dead level was his strong suit, you understand; and when it come to that, Smiley

would ante up money on him as long as he had a red. Smiley was monstrous proud of his frog, and well he might be, for fellers that had traveled and been everywheres all said he laid over any frog that ever *they* see.

Well, Smiley kep' the beast in a little lattice box, and he used to fetch him down town sometimes and lay for a bet. One day a feller —a stranger in the camp, he was—come acrost him with his box, and says:

"What might it be that you've got in the box?"

And Smiley says, sorter indifferent-like, "It might be a parrot, or it might be a canary, maybe, but it ain't—its only just a frog."

And the feller took it, and looked at it careful, and turned it round this way and that, and says, "H'm—so 'tis. Well, what's *he* good for?"

"Well," Smiley says, easy and careless, "he's good enough for *one* thing, I should judge—he can outjump any frog in Calaveras county."

The feller took the box again, and took another long, particular look, and give it back to Smiley, and says, very deliberate, "Well," he says, "I don't see no p'ints about that frog that's any better'n any other frog."

"Maybe you don,'t," Smiley says. "Maybe you understand frogs and maybe you don't understand 'em; maybe you've had experience, and maybe you ain't only a amature, as it were. Anyways, I've got *my* opinion, and I'll resk forty dollars that he can outjump any frog in Calaveras county."

And the feller studied a minute, and then says, kinder sad like, "Well, I'm only a stranger here, and I ain't got no frog; but if I had a frog, I'd bet you."

And then Smiley says, "That's all right—that's all right—if you'll hold my box a minute, I'll go and get you a frog." And so the feller took the box, and put up his forty dollars along with Smiley's, and set down to wait.

So he set there a good while thinking and thinking to hisself, and then he got the frog out and prized his mouth open and took a teaspoon and filled him full of quail shot—filled him pretty near up to his chin—and set him on the floor. Smiley he went to the swamp and slopped around in the mud for a long time, and finally he ketched a frog, and fetched him in, and give him to this feller, and says:

"Now, if you're ready, set him alongside of Dan'l, with his forepaws just even with Dan'l's, and I'll give the word." Then he says, "One—two—three—*git!*" and him and the feller touched up the frogs from behind, and the new frog hopped off lively, but Dan'l give a heave, and hysted up his shoulders—so—like a Frenchman, but it warn't no use—he couldn't budge; he was planted as solid as a church, and he couldn't no more stir than if he was anchored out. Smiley was a good deal surprised, and he was disgusted too, but he didn't have no idea what the matter was, of course.

The feller took the money and started away; and when he was going out at the door, he sorter jerked his thumb over his shoulder —so—at Dan'l, and says again, very deliberate, "Well," he says, "*I* don't see no p'ints about that frog that's any better'n any other frog."

Smiley he stood scratching his head and looking down at Dan'l a long time, and at last he says, "I do wonder what in the nation that frog throw'd off for—I wonder if there ain't something the matter with him—he 'pears to look mighty baggy, somehow." And he ketched Dan'l by the nap of the neck, and hefted him, and says, "Why blame my cats if he don't weigh five pound!" and turned him upside down and he belched out a double handful of shot. And then he see how it was, and he was the maddest man—he set the frog down and took out after that feller, but he never ketched him. And——"

[Here Simon Wheeler heard his name called from the front yard, and got up to see what was wanted.] And turning to me as he moved away, he said: "Just set where you are, stranger, and rest easy—I ain't going to be gone a second."

But, by your leave, I did not think that a continuation of the enterprising vagabond *Jim* Smiley would be likely to afford me much information concerning the Rev. *Leonidas W.* Smiley, and so I started away.

At the door I met the sociable Wheeler returning, and he button-holed me and re-commenced:

"Well, thish-yer Smiley had a yaller one-eyed cow that didn't have no tail, only just a short stump like a bannanner, and——"

However, lacking both time and inclination, I did not wait to hear about the afflicted cow, but took my leave.

Now let the learned look upon this picture and say
if iconoclasm can further go:

[From the *Revue des Deux Mondes*, of July 15th, 1872.]

LA GRENOUILLE SANTEUSE DU COMTE
DE CALAVERAS.

"—Il y avait une fois ici un individu connu sous le nom de Jim
Smiley: c'était dans l'hiver de 49, peut-être bien au printemps de
50, je ne me rappelle pas exactement. Ce qui me fait croire que
c'était l'un ou l'autre, c'est que je me souviens que le grand bief
n'était pas achevé lorsqu'il arriva au camp pour la première fois,
mais de toutes façons il était l'homme le plus friand de paris qui
se pût voir, pariant sur tout ce qui se présentait, quand il pouvait
trouver un adversaire, et, quand il n'en trouvait pas il passait de
côté opposé. Tout ce qui convenait à l'autre lui convenait: pourvu
qu'il eût un pari, Smiley était satisfait. Et il avait une chance! une
chance inouie: presque toujours il gagnait. Il faut dire qu'il était
toujours prêt à s'exposer, qu'on ne pouvait mentionner la moindre
chose sans que ce gaillard offrît de parier là-dessus n'importe quoi
et de prendre le côté que l'on voudrait, comme je vous le disais tout
à l'heure. S'il y avait des courses, vous le trouviez riche ou ruiné
à la fin; s'il y avait un combat de chiens, il apportait son enjeu; il
l'apportait pour un combat de chats, pour un combat de coqs;
—parbleu! si vous aviez deux oiseaux sur une haie, il vous aurait
offert de parier lequel s'envolerait le premier, et, s'il y avait *meeting*
au camp, il venait parier régulièrement pour le curé Walker, qu'il

jugeait être le meilleur prédicateur des environs, et qui l'était en effet, et un brave homme. Il aurait rencontre une punaise de bois en chemin, qu'il aurait parié sur le temps qu'il lui faudrait pour aller où elle voudrait aller, et, si vous l'aviez pris au mot, il aurait suivi la punaise jusqu'au Mexique, sans se soucier d'aller si loin, ni du temps qu'il y perdrait. Une fois la femme du curé Walker fut très malade pendant longtemps, il semblait qu'on ne la sauverait pas ; mais un matin le curé arrive, et Smiley lui demande comment elle va, et il dit qu'elle est bien mieux, grâce à l'infinie miséricorde, tellement mieux qu'avec la bénédiction de la Providence elle s'en tirerait, et voilà que, sans y penser, Smiley répond :—Eh bien ! je gage deux et demi qu'elle mourra tout de même.

"Ce Smiley avait une jument que les gars appelaient le bidet du quart d'heure, mais seulement pour plaisanter, vous comprenez, parce que, bien entendu, elle était plus *vite* que ça ! Et il avait coutume de gagner de l'argent avec cette bête, quoiqu'elle fût poussive, cornarde, toujours prise d'asthme, de coliques ou de consomption, ou de quelque chose d'approchant. On lui donnait 2 ou 300 *yards* au départ, puis on la dépassait sans peine ; mais jamais à la fin elle ne manquait de s'échauffer, de s'exaspérer, et elle arrivait, s'écartant, se défendant, ses jambes grêles en l'air devant les obstacles, quelquefois les évitant et faisant avec cela plus de poussière qu'aucun cheval, plus de bruit surtout avec ses éternumens et reniflemens,—crac ! elle arrivait donc toujours première d'une tête, aussi juste qu'on peut le mesurer. Et il avait un petit bouledogue qui, à le voir, ne valait pas un sou ; on aurait cru que parier contre lui c'était voler, tant il était ordinaire : mais aussitôt les enjeux faits, il devenait un autre chien. Sa mâchoire inférieure commençait à ressortir comme un gaillard d'avant, ses dents se découvraient brillantes commes des fournaises, et un chien pouvait le taquiner, l'exciter, le mordre, le jeter deux ou trois fois par-dessus son épaule, André Jackson, c'était le nom du chien, André Jackson prenait cela tranquillement, comme s'il ne se fût jamais attendu à autre chose, et quand les paris étaient doublés et redoublés contre lui, il vous saisissait l'autre chien juste à l'articulation de la jambe de derrière, et il ne la lâchait plus, non pas qu'il la mâchât, vous concevez, mais il s'y serait tenu pendu jusqu'à ce qu'on jetât l'éponge en l'air, fallût-il attendre un an. Smiley gagnait toujours avec cette bête-là ; malheureusement ils ont fini par dresser un chien qui n'avait pas de pattes de derrière, parce qu'on les avait sciées, et quand les choses furent au point qu'il voulait, et qu'il en vint à se jeter sur son morceau favori, le pauvre chien comprit en un instant qu'on s'était moqué de lui, et que l'autre le tenait. Vou n'avez jamais vu personne avoir l'air plus penaud et plus découragé ; il ne fit aucun effort pour gagner le combat et fut rudement secoué, de sorte que, regardant Smiley comme pour lui dire : — Mon cœur est brisé, c'est ta faute ; pourquoi m'avoir livré à un chien qui n'a pas de pattes de derrière, puisque c'est par là que je les bats ? — il s'en alla en clopinant, et se coucha pour mourir. Ah ! c'était un bon chien, cet André Jackson, et il se serait fait un nom, s'il avait vécu, car il y avait de l'etoffe en lui, il avait du génie, je la sais, bien que de grandes occasions lui aient manqué ; mais il est impossible de supposer qu'un chien capable de se battre comme lui, certaines circonstances étant données, ait manqué de talent. Je me sens triste toutes les fois que je pense à son dernier combat et au dénoûment qu'il a eu. Eh bien! ce Smiley nourrissait des terriers à rats, et des coqs de combat, et des chats, et toute sorte de choses, au point qu'il était toujours en mesure de vous tenir tête, et qu'avec sa rage de paris on n'avait plus de repos. Il attrapa un jour une grenouille et l'emporta chez lui, disant qu'il prétendait faire son éducation; vous me croirez si vous voulez, mais pendant trois mois il n'a rien fait que lui apprendre à sauter dans une cour retirée de sa maison. Et je vous réponds qu'il avait réussi. Il lui donnait un petit coup par derrière, et l'instant d'après vous voyiez la grenouille tourner en l'air comme un beignet au-dessus de la poêle, faire une culbute, quelquefois deux, lorsqu'elle était bien partie, et retomber sur ses pattes comme un chat. Il l'avait dressée dans l'art de gober des mouches, et l'y exerçait continuellement, si bien qu'une mouche, du plus loin qu'elle apparaissait, était une mouche perdue. Smiley avait coutume de dire que tout ce qui manquait à une grenouille, c'était l'éducation, qu'avec l'éducation elle pouvait faire presque tout, et je le crois. Tenez, je l'ai vu poser Daniel Webster là sur se plancher, —Daniel Webster était le nom de la grenouille, —et lui chanter : —Des mouches! Daniel, des mouches! —En un clin d'œil, Daniel avait bondi et saisi une mouche ici sur le comptoir, puis sauté de nouveau par terre, où il re_tait vraiment à se gratter la tête avec sa patte de derrière, comme s'il n'avait pas eu la moindre idée de sa supériorité. Jamais vous n'avez grenouille vu de aussi modeste, aussi naturelle, douée comme elle l'était! Et quand il s'agissait de sauter purement et simplement sur terrain plat, elle faisait plus de chemin en un saut qu'aucune bête de son espèce que vous puissiez connaître.

Sauter à plat, c'était son fort! Quand il s'agissait de cela, Smiley entassait les enjeux sur elle tant qu'il lui, restait un rouge liard. Il faut le reconnaître, Smiley était monstrueusement fièr de sa grenouille, et il en avait le droit, car des gens qui avaient voyagé, qui avaient tout vu, disaient qu'on lui ferait injure de la comparer à une autre; de façon que Smiley gardait Daniel dans une petite boîte à clairevoie qu'il emporta et parfois à la ville pour quelque pari.

"Un jour, un individu étranger au camp l'arrête avec sa boite et lui dit:—Qu'est-ce que vous avez donc serré là dedans?

"Smiley dit d'un air indifférent:—Cela pourrait être une perroquet ou un serin, mais ce n'est rien de pareil, ce n'est qu'une grenouille.

"L'individu la prend, la regarde avec soin, la tourne d'un côté et de l'autre puss il dit.—Tiens! en effet! A quoi est-elle bonne?

"—Mon Dieu! répond Smiley, toujours d'un air dégagé, elle est bonne pour une chose à mon avis, elle peut battre en sautant toute grenouille du comté de Calaveras.

"L'individu reprend la boîte, l'examine de nouveau longuement, et la rend à Smiley en disant d'un air délibéré:—Eh bien! je ne vois pas que cette grenouille ait rien de mieux qu'aucune grenouille.

"—Possible que vous ne le voyiez pas, dit Smiley, possible que vous vous entendiez en grenouilles, possible que vous ne vous y entendez point, possible que vous ayez de l'expérience, et possible que vous ne soyez qu'un amateur. De toute manière, je parie quarante dollars qu'elle battra en sautant n'importe quelle grenouille du comté de Calaveras.

"L'individu réfléchit une seconde et dit comme attristé:—Je ne suis qu'un étranger ici, je n'ai pas de grenouille ; mais, si j'en avais une, je tiendrais le pari.

"—Fort bien ! répond Smiley. Rien de plus facile. Si vous voulez tenir ma boîte une minute, j'irai vous chercher une grenouille.— Voilà donc l'individu qui garde la boîte, qui met ses quarante dollars sur ceux de Smiley et qui attend. Il attend assez longtemps, réfléchissant tout seul, et figurez-vous qu'il prend Daniel, lui ouvre la bouche de force et avec une cuiller à thé l'emplit de menu plomb de chasse, mais l'emplit jusqu'au menton, puis il le pose par terre. Smiley pendant ce temps était à barboter dans une mare. Finalement il attrape une grenouille, l'apporte à cet individu et dit :— Maintenant, si vous êtes prêt, mettez-la tout contre Daniel, avec leurs pattes de devant sur la même ligne, et je donnerai le signal ;— puis il ajoute :—Un, deux, trois, sautez !

"Lui et l'individu touchent leurs grenouilles par derrière, et la grenouille neuve se met à sautiller, mais Daniel se soulève lourdement, hausse les épaules ainsi, comme un Français ; à quoi bon ? il ne pouvait bouger, il était planté solide comme une enclume, il n'avançait pas plus que si on l'eût mis à l'ancre. Smiley fut surpris et dégoûté, mais il ne se doutait pas du tour, bien entendu. L'individu empoche l'argent, s'en va, et en s'en allant est-ce-qu'il de donne pas un coup de pouce par-dessus l'épaule, comme ça, au pauvre Daniel, en disant de son air délibéré :—Eh bien ! je ne vois pas que cette grenuoille ait rien de mieux qu'une autre.

"Smiley se gratta longtemps la tête, les yeux fixés sur Daniel, jusqu'à ce qu'enfin il dit :— Je me demande comment diable il se fait que cette bête ait refusé . . . Est-ce qu'elle aurait quelque chose? . . . On croirait qu'elle est enflée.

"Il empoigne Daniel par la peau du cou, le souléve et dit:—Le loup me croque, s'il ne pèse pas cinq livres.

"Il le retourne, et le malheureux crache deux poignées de plomb. Quand Smiley reconnut ce qui en était, il fut comme fou. Vous le voyez d'ici poser sa grenouille par terre et courir après cet individu, mais il ne le rattrapa jamais, et . . .

[Translation of the above back from the French.]

THE FROG JUMPING OF THE COUNTY OF CALAVERAS.

It there was one time here an individual known under the name of Jim Smiley; it was in the winter of '49, possibly well at the spring of '50, I no me recollect not exactly. This which me makes to believe that it was the one or the other, it is that I shall remember that the grand flume is not achieved when he arrives at the camp for the first time, but of all sides he was the man the most fond of to bet which one have seen, betting upon all that which is presented, when he could find an adversary; and when he not of it could not, he passed to the side opposed. All that which convenienced to the other, to him convenienced also; seeing that he had a

bet, Smiley was satisfied. And he had a chance! a chance
even worthless; nearly always he gained. It must to say
that he was always near to himself expose, but one no
could mention the least thing without that this gaillard
offered to bet the bottom, no matter what, and to take
the side that one him would, as I you it said all at the
hour (tout à l'heure). If it there was of races, you him
find rich or ruined at the end; if it there is a combat of
dogs, he bring his bet; he himself laid always for a
combat of cats, for a combat of cocks;—by-blue! If you
have see two birds upon a fence, he you should have
offered of to bet which of those birds shall fly the first;
and if there is *meeting* at the camp (*meeting* au camp) he
comes to bet regularly for the curé Walker, which he
judged to be the best predicator of the neighborhood
(prédicateur des environs) and which he was in effect,
and a brave man. He would encounter a bug of wood in
the road, whom he will bet upon the time which he shall
take to go where she would go—and if you him have
take at the word, he will follow the bug as far as Mexique, without himself caring to go so far; neither of the
time which he there lost. One time the woman of the
curé Walker is very sick during long time, it seemed
that one not her saved not; but one morning the curé

arrives, and Smiley him demanded how she goes, and he said that she is well better, grace to the infinite misery (lui demande comment elle va, et il dit qu'elle est bien mieux, grâce à l'infinie misèricorde) so much better that with the benediction of the Providence she herself of it would pull out (elle s'en tierarait); and behold that without there thinking Smiley responds: "Well, I gage two-and-half that she will die all of same."

This Smiley had an animal which the boys called the nag of the quarter of hour, but solely for pleasantry, you comprehend, because, well understand, she was more fast as that! [Now why that exclamation?—M. T.] And it was custom of to gain of the silver with this beast, notwithstanding she was poussive, cornarde, always taken of asthma, of colics or of consumption, or something of approaching. One him would give two or three hundred yards at the departure, then one him passed without pain; but never at the last she not fail of herself èchauffer, of herself exasperate, and she arrives herself écartant, se dèfendant, her legs grêles in the air before the obstacles, sometimes them elevating and making with this more of dust than any horse, more of noise above with his éternumens and reniflemens— crac! she arrives then always first by one head, as just as one can it measure. And he had a small bull dog (boule dogue!) who, to him see, no value, not a cent; one would believe that to bet against him it was to steal, so much he was ordinary; but as soon as the game made, she becomes another dog. Her jaw inferior commence to project like a deck of before, his teeth themselves discover brilliant like some furnaces, and a dog could him tackle (le taquiner), him excite, him murder (le mordre), him throw two or three times over his shoulder, André Jackson—this was the name of the dog—André Jackson takes that tranquilly, as if he not himself was never expecting other thing, and when the bets were doubled and redoubled against him, he you seize the other dog just at the articulation of the leg of behind, and he not it leave more, not that he it masticate, you conceive, but he himself there shall be holding during until that one throws the sponge in the air, must he wait a year. Smiley gained always with this beast-là; unhappily they have finished by elevating a dog who no had not of feet of behind, because one them had sawed; and when things were at the point that he would, and that he came to himself throw upon his morsel favorite, the poor dog comprehended in an instant that he himself was deceived in him, and that the other dog him had.

You no have never see person having the air more penaud and more discouraged; he not made no effort to gain the combat, and was rudely shucked.

Eh bien! this Smiley nourished some terriers à rats, and some cocks of combat, and some cats, and all sorts of things; and with his rage of betting one no had more of repose. He trapped one day a frog and him imported with him (et l'emporta chez lui) saying that he pretended to make his education. You me believe if you will, but during three months he not has nothing done but to him apprehend to jump (apprendre à sauter) in a court retired of her mansion (de sa maison). And I you respond that he have succeeded. He him gives a small blow by behind, and the instant after you shall see the frog turn in the air like a grease-biscuit, make one summersault, sometimes two, when she was well started, and re-fall upon his feet like a cat. He him had accomplished in the art of to gobble the flies (gober des mouches), and him there exercised continually—so well that a fly at the most far that she appeared was a fly lost. Smiley had custom to say that all which lacked to a frog it was the education, but with the education she could do nearly all—and I him believe. Tenez, I him have seen posed Daniel Webster there upon this plank—Daniel

Webster was the name of the frog—and to him sing, "Some flies, Daniel, some flies!"—in a flash of the eye Daniel had bounded and seized a fly here upon the counter, then jumped anew at the earth, where he rested truly to himself scratch the head with his behind foot, as if he no had not the least idea of his superiority. Never you not have seen frog as modest, as natural, sweet as she was. And when he himself agitated to jump purely and simply upon plain earth, she does more ground in one jump than any beast of his species than you can know. To jump plain—this was his strong. When he himself agitated for that, Smiley multiplied the bets upon her as long as there to him remained a red. It must to know, Smiley was monstrously proud of his frog, and he of it was right, for some men who were traveled, who had all seen, said that they to him would be injurious to him compare to another frog. Smiley guarded Daniel in a little box latticed which he carried bytimes to the village for some bet.

One day an individual stranger at the camp him arrested with his box and him said:

"What is this that you have then shut up there within?"

Smiley said, with an air indifferent:

"That could be a paroquet, or a syringe (ou un serin), but this no is nothing of such, it not is but a frog."

The individual it took, it regarded with care, it turned from one side and from the other, then he said:

"Tiens! in effect!—At what is she good?"

"My God!" respond Smiley, always with an air disengaged, "she is good for one thing, to my notice (à mon avis), she can batter in jumping (elle peut batter en sautant) all frogs of the county of Calaveras."

The individual re-took the box, it examined of new longly, and it rendered to Smiley in saying with an air deliberate:

"Eh bien! I no saw not that that frog had nothing of better than each frog." (Je ne vois pas que cette grenouille ait rien de mieux qu'aucune grenouille.) [If that isn't grammar gone to seed, then I count myself no judge.—M. T.]

"Possible that you not it saw not," said Smiley, "possible that you—you comprehend frogs; possible that you not you there comprehend nothing; possible that you had of the experience, and possible that you not be but an amateur. Of all manner (De toute manière) I bet forty dollars that she batter in jumping no matter which frog of the county of Calaveras."

The individual reflected a second, and said like sad:

"I not am but a stranger here, I no have not a frog; but if I of it had one, I would embrace the bet."

"Strong well!" respond Smiley; "nothing of more facility. If you will hold my box a minute, I go you to search a frog (j'irai vous chercher)."

Behold, then, the individual, who guards the box, who puts his forty dollars upon those of Smiley, and who attends (et qui attend). He attended enough long-times, reflecting all solely. And figure you that he takes Daniel, him opens the mouth by force and with a tea-spoon him fills with shot of the hunt, even him fills just to the chin, then he him puts by the earth. Smiley during these times was at slopping in a swamp. Finally he trapped (attrape) a frog, him carried to that individual, and said:

"Now if you be ready, put him all against Daniel, with their before feet upon the same line, and I give the signal"—then he added: "One, two, three—advance!"

Him and the individual touched their frogs by behind, and the frog new put to jump smartly, but Daniel himself lifted ponderously, exalted the shoulders thus, like a Frenchman—to what good? he not could budge, he is planted solid like a church, he not advance no more than if one him had put at the anchor.

Smiley was surprised and disgusted, but he not himself doubted not of the turn being intended (mais il ne se doutait pas du tour, bien entendu). The individual empocketed the silver, himself with it went, and of it himself in going is it that he no gives not a jerk of thumb over the shoulder—like that—at the poor Daniel, in saying with his air deliberate—(L'individu empoche l'argent, s'en va et en s'en allant est ce qu'il ne donne pas un coup de pouce par-dessus l'épaule, comme ca, au pauvre Daniel, endisant de son air délibéré):

"Eh bien! *I no see not that that frog has nothing of better than another.*"

Smiley himself scratched longtimes the head, the eyes fixed upon Daniel, until that which at last he said:

"I me demand how the devil it makes itself that this beast has refused. Is it that she had something? One would believe that she is stuffed."

He grasped Daniel by the skin of the neck, him lifted and said:

"The wolf me bite if he no weigh not five pounds."

He him reversed and the unhappy belched two handfuls of shot (et le malheureurs, etc.). When Smiley recognized how it was, he was like mad. He deposited his frog by the earth and ran after that individual, but he not him caught never.

Such is the Jumping Frog, to the distorted French eye. I claim that I never put together such an odious mixture of bad grammar and delirium tremens in my life. And what has a poor foreigner like me done, to be abused and misrepresented like this? When I say, "Well, I don't see no p'ints about that frog that's any better'n any other frog," is it kind, is it just, for this Frenchman to try to make it appear that I said, "Eh bien! I no saw not that that frog had nothing of better than each frog?" I have no heart to write more. I never felt so about anything before.

Mark Twain

Hartford, March, 1875.

PRIVATE HISTORY OF THE "JUMPING FROG" STORY

FIVE OR SIX YEARS AGO A LADY FROM FINLAND asked me to tell her a story in our negro dialect, so that she could get an idea of what that variety of speech was like. I told her one of Hopkinson Smith's negro stories, and gave her a copy of *Harper's Monthly* containing it. She translated it for a Swedish newspaper, but by an oversight named me as the author of it instead of Smith. I was very sorry for that, because I got a good lashing in the Swedish press, which would have fallen to his share but for that mistake; for it was shown that Boccaccio had told that very story, in his curt and meagre fashion, five hundred years before Smith took hold of it and made a good and tellable thing out of it.

I have always been sorry for Smith. But my own turn has come now. A few weeks ago Professor Van Dyke, of Princeton, asked this question:

"Do you know how old your Jumping Frog story is?"

And I answered:

"Yes—forty-five years. The thing happened in Calaveras County in the spring of 1849."

"No; it happened earlier—a couple of thousand years earlier; it is a Greek story."

I was astonished—and hurt. I said:

"I am willing to be a literary thief if it has been so ordained; I am even willing to be caught robbing the ancient dead alongside of

Hopkinson Smith, for he is my friend and a good fellow, and I think would be as honest as any one if he could do it without occasioning remark; but I am not willing to antedate his crimes by fifteen hundred years. I must ask you to knock off part of that."

But the professor was not chaffing; he was in earnest, and could not abate a century. He named the Greek author, and offered to get the book and send it to me and the college text-book containing the English translation also. I thought I would like the translation best, because Greek makes me tired. January 30th he sent me the English version, and I will presently insert it in this article. It is my Jumping Frog tale in every essential. It is not strung out as I have strung it out, but it is all there.

To me this is very curious and interesting. Curious for several reasons. For instance:

I heard the story told by a man who was not telling it to his hearers as a thing new to them, but as a thing which *they had witnessed and would remember.* He was a dull person, and ignorant; he had no gift as a story-teller, and no invention; in his mouth this episode was merely history—history and statistics; and the gravest sort of history, too; he was entirely serious, for he was dealing with what to him were austere facts, and they interested him solely because they *were* facts; he was drawing on his memory, not his mind; he saw no humor in his tale, neither did his listeners; neither he nor they ever smiled or laughed; in my time I have not attended a more solemn conference. To him and to his fellow gold-miners there were just two things in the story that were worth considering. One was the smartness of the stranger in taking in its hero, Jim Smiley, with a loaded frog; and the other was the stranger's deep knowledge of a frog's nature—for he knew (as the narrator asserted and the listeners conceded) that a frog *likes shot* and is always ready to eat it. Those men discussed those two points, and those only. They were hearty in their admiration of them, and none of the party was aware that a first-rate story had been told in a first-rate way, and that it was brimful of a quality whose presence they never suspected—humor.

Now, then, the interesting question is, *did* the frog episode happen in Angel's Camp in the spring of '49, as told in my hearing that day in the fall of 1865? I am perfectly sure that it did. I am also sure that its duplicate happened in Bœotia a couple of thousand years ago. I think it must be a case of history actually repeating itself, and not a case of a good story floating down the ages and surviving because too good to be allowed to perish.

I would now like to have the reader examine the Greek story and the story told by the dull and solemn Californian, and observe how exactly alike they are in essentials.

[*Translation.*]

THE ATHENIAN AND THE FROG.

An Athenian once fell in with a Bœotian who was sitting by the road side looking at a frog. Seeing the other approach, the Bœotian said his was a remarkable frog, and asked if he would agree to start a contest of frogs, on condition that he whose frog jumped farthest should receive a large sum of money. The Athenian replied that he would if the other would fetch him a frog, for the lake was near. To this he agreed, and when he was gone the Athenian took the frog, and, opening its mouth, poured some stones into its stomach, so that it did not indeed seem larger than before, but could not jump. The Bœotian soon returned with the other frog, and the contest began. The second frog first was pinched, and jumped moderately; then they pinched the Bœotian frog. And he gathered himself for a leap, and used the utmost effort, but he could not move his body the least. So the Athenian departed with the money. When he was gone the Bœotian, wondering what was the matter with the frog, lifted him up and examined him. And being turned upside down, he opened his mouth and vomited out the stones.

Sidgwick: *Greek Prose Composition*

The resemblances are deliciously exact. There you have the wily Bœotian and the wily Jim Smiley waiting—two thousand years apart—and waiting, each equipped with his frog and "laying" for the stranger. A contest is proposed—for money. The Athenian would take a chance "if the other would fetch him a frog"; the Yankee says: "I'm only a stranger here, and I ain't got no frog; but if I had a frog I'd bet you." The wily Bœotian and the wily Californian, with that vast gulf of two thousand years between, retire eagerly and go frogging in the marsh; the Athenian and the Yankee remain behind and work a base advantage, the one with pebbles, the other with shot. Presently the contest began. In the one case "they pinched the Bœotian frog"; in the other, "him and the feller touched up the frogs from behind." The Bœotian frog "gathered himself for a leap" (you can just *see* him!), "but could not move his body in the least"; the Californian frog "give a heave, but it warn't no use—he couldn't budge." In both the ancient and the modern cases the strangers departed with the money. The Bœotian and the Californian wonder what is the matter with their frogs; they lift them and examine; they turn them upside down and out spills the informing ballast.

Yes, the resemblances are curiously exact. I used to tell the story of the Jumping Frog in San Francisco, and presently Artemus Ward came along and wanted it to help fill out a little book which he was about to publish; so I wrote it out and sent it to his publisher, Carleton; but Carleton thought the book had enough matter in it, so he gave the story to Henry Clapp as a present, and Clapp put it in his *Saturday Press*, and it killed that paper with a suddenness that was beyond praise. At least the paper died with that issue, and none but envious people have ever tried to rob me of the honor and credit of killing it. The "Jumping Frog" was the first piece of writing of mine that spread itself through the newspapers and brought me into public notice. Consequently, the *Saturday Press* was a cocoon and I the worm in it; also, I was the gay-colored literary moth which its death set free. This simile has been used before.

Early in '66 the "Jumping Frog" was issued in book form, with other sketches of mine. A year or two later Madame Blanc translated it into French and published it in the *Revue des Deux Mondes*, but the result was not what should have been expected, for the *Revue* struggled along and pulled through, and is alive yet. I think the fault must have been in the translation. I ought to have translated it myself. I think so because I examined into the matter and finally retranslated the sketch from the French back into English, to see what the trouble was; that is, to see just what sort of a focus the French people got upon it. Then the mystery was explained. In French the story is too confused, and chaotic, and unreposeful, and ungrammatical, and insane; consequently it could only cause grief and sickness—it could not kill. A glance at my re-translation will show the reader that this must be true.

It may be that there are people who can translate better than I can, but I am not acquainted with them.

So ends the private and public history of the Jumping Frog of Calaveras County, an incident which has this unique feature about it—that it is both old and new, a "chestnut" and not a "chestnut"; for it was original when it happened two thousand years ago, and was again original when it happened in California in our own time.

Samuel Clemens

The text for this edition of THE JUMPING FROG is from "MARK TWAIN'S SKETCHES, *NEW AND OLD,*" as it was first published in complete form, 1875, the American Publishing Co. It contains three versions of this notorious and celebrated tale, the original (1865), translated into the French, and then "restored to the English after martyrdom in the French." The afterword, THE PRIVATE PRINTING OF THE "JUMPING FROG" STORY, by Samuel Clemens, first appeared in the North American Review #158 (April 1894). The fifteen wood engravings were originally printed at Cheloniidæ Press, One Cottage St., Easthampton, Massachusetts by Harold P. McGrath. The type is Centaur and Arrighi set by Mackenzie-Harris.

ILLUSTRATOR

Alan James Robinson

The wood engravings are by the award-winning artist and owner of Press of the Sea Turtle, formerly Cheloniidae Press, of Easthampton, Massachusetts. The press was founded in 1979. The editions are limited and printed on letterpress. The predominant content theme of the books is related to the animal world, but within that context the books are as varied as *The Birds and Beasts of Shakespeare, An Odd Bestiary,* and *The Raven.*